I0520087

Pass,
Passed,
Past

Jean Light Willis

Copyright © 2013 by Jean Light Willis
Publication date, November 21, 2013

ISBN: 978-0-982-91147-1

All rights reserved. No part of this book may be reproduced
or transmitted in any form or by any means, electronic or
mechanical, including photocopying, recording, or by any
information storage and retrieval system, without
permission in writing from the copyright owner.

This book was printed in the United States of America.

Senesis Word Publisher

Phone: 904-687-1865   **Cell:** 574-265-3386

FAX: 904-825-0222

Website: www.Ho2Jo.com

Email: Senesisword@yahoo.com

PassWillis13C13N

Pass, Passed, Past

is dedicated to

my high school English teacher

and dear friend

Miss Elizabeth Stone

of Roanoke, Virginia

Pass 1

"Pass."

"Pass."

"Pass."

"Well, that makes Lillian dummy," Gertrude noted.

"I'll go check the oven," Lillian said as she quickly fanned her cards on the table and left for the kitchen.

"She always does that," spat Penelope, trying to cover Lillian's cards, waiting for Stella to lead.

"What's trumps?" asked Stella as she rummaged in her enormous purse looking for her cigarette lighter.

"Spades. Four spades. Pay attention, Stella!" snapped Penelope.

"You know Lillian doesn't want you to smoke in here, although I don't see why she should care since her animals and her grandchildren keep it so interesting," Penelope added.

Just at that moment there was a loud clap of thunder. Two cats and a dog collided as they scampered to hide under the sofa, knocking over a vase of pussy willows, forsythia and camellias from the end table.

As Lillian rushed from the kitchen Gertrude whispered, "I'll help," glancing at her hand before stooping to retrieve the promises of spring.

"Aw, it's the pink vase Harold gave you," Stella noted.

"Too many pieces to glue back together," said a tearful Lillian as she mopped up the water with her dishtowel.

"I really didn't like that pink vase but I kept it because Harold gave it to me," she guiltily confessed.

Gertrude noticed the hodgepodge of things that had probably been kept because they were gifts from Lillian's loved ones, thinking it was an interesting room despite the overflow of memorabilia. Sculpture made by talented grandchildren was displayed among her mother's renowned antique doll collection. Family pictures told of a hundred years of special events. Potted plants filled all available spaces.

"Well girls, we still have four pussies, *for-syphilis* and a camellia," said Stella as she held up the still dripping sprigs.

They collapsed with laughter as the tears rolled down their faces sharing their memory of a childhood mispronunciation of forsythia. They had been friends since grammar school and shared many memories.

Gert realized that after being together for a few minutes they were no longer aware of each other's wrinkles or other signs of aging. Like sisters, they were aware of each other's faults and talents but they had a bond that survived even occasional rivalry.

Cheerfully four pairs of hands picked shards of glass and plant parts from the drenched carpet as more thunder boomed. Despite creaking knees they rose as the lights went out and the rain began in earnest.

"Since the electricity is out and the casserole isn't done, let's just have more chips and dip." Lillian said.

"I'll open another bottle of wine," offered Stella.

Lillian passed a tray of homemade snacks to Penelope saying, "Honey, I know you believe you can't be too thin or too rich, but try these special pecans fixed by Gert. They are from the tree in her yard we used to climb when we wanted to spy on the boys next door."

"These pecans really taste good, Gert - made with some secret ingredients? How about the recipe?" said Stella, as she filled the wine glasses again.

"Lillian is the expert. She uses bouillon cubes, sea salt and Worcester sauce. If you and Penny want, she'll write it down for you," Gertrude volunteered.

Lillian's plump face beamed, as Penelope looked for a scrap of paper and produced an envelope saying, "Here write on this."

Penelope had pulled out two envelopes, handing one to Lillian as she held up the other saying she had just received it from her hippie daughter, Phyllis.

"She'll be home soon bringing a surprise guest! She didn't say who, when, why or for how long," she said. She sounded exasperated. "I remember her last visit. Trying to plan menus for Phyllis and three vegetarians was just too much. And Howard was furious. They smoked pot last time as they planned a protest rally. I wonder what she is protesting this time," she said and rolled her eyes.

"Phyllis probably inherited the protest gene from one of those famous revolutionaries you brag about," thought Gertrude.

"Maybe you could send Phyllis's guest to stay in my apartment and feed my cats while I'm in the clinic," stated Stella.

Gertrude wondered what Stella was having nipped or tucked this time in the clinic, but didn't ask knowing Stella didn't like to discuss doctors or health or growing older. Her mind was on how the storm might be affecting her roof. During the last big storm a large limb from the infamous pecan tree had fallen on her roof causing some expensive repairs. She was glad to see the sky begin to lighten.

"The storm has passed over, but barely before we pass out." Stella said.

"How will we get home? None of us should drive," said Penny.

The sun came out just as Lillian's oldest daughter, Maude, on her way home from work, came by to check on her mom. She offered to give the girls a ride home adding, "I'll pick you up in the morning when Mom and I go to the curb market. You can come back for your cars."

Penny donned her raincoat while Stella gathered her belongings and drank one more glass of wine.

Before dashing to Maude's car, Gert stopped to help Lillian take a few glasses to the kitchen when she noticed a small white card on the floor. Handing it to Lillian Gert read, "Appointment April 1, 1 p.m., Dr. John Gibson."

"Now, who has an appointment with our oncologist?" Lillian said with a look of shock on her face.

"Let's wait and find out tomorrow morning," Gert suggested as she hugged her friend and rushed to join the others.

Pass 2

Gert could see whitecaps in the sound as Maude drove her home along Front Street which was beginning to flood. As they rounded the corner, Fred could be seen on Gert's porch wagging his tail in welcome. She was relieved to see no major damage, only sticks and leaves blown about, but she knew the storm was not over. It was reported that this was a front passing through so more rain was predicted.

No sooner had she thanked Maude and let Fred and herself inside than the wind picked up and it began to pour. She headed into the kitchen listening to creaks and groans of the friendly ghosts who lived with her. Based on past experience she didn't expect to have power until the storm passed. She made sure Fred had food and water and decided she was hungry too.

She took a sandwich and milk with her into the library where she lit a fire to ward off the chill and dampness creeping into the old house. The library was her favorite room furnished with her mother's desk, a few good lamps, her great grandmother's trunk that also served as a table and two very old red leather chairs. The bookshelves rose to the ceiling filled with volumes that had been collected over many years. Some were her grandfather's, some her mother's or her brother's, and she had continued to add her favorites. Many had been gifts with notes to the recipient on a special occasion such as graduation, birthday or Christmas written on the flyleaf. What a warm feeling it was to share in the love expressed through these gifts upon a milestone in their life.

She was all alone now except for her friends all in their mid seventies, they had shared many dreams, attitudes and secrets since they became friends in the fifth grade. Each would have been lonely except for their strong friendship with each other, Gert thought. Penny does have her grumpy husband, Lillian has her children, and Stella has her cats then she remembered the mysterious appointment card.

She pulled her chair closer to the firelight so she could see to read it again.

"Could it belong to Penny- Penny, who hated going to a doctor, had said that she hadn't seen one in a couple of years? Could it be Stella's- Stella, who refused to admit to getting older, often getting nips and tucks here and there? Who might have dropped it?"

Suddenly a brilliant light exploded with the earsplitting crash of giant cymbals!

She and Fred both jumped.

"That was a close one," she said.

Fred whimpered and she said, "It's all right, Baby."

As she caught her breath, she became aware of the acrid smell of burning plastic or wire.

Heart pounding she raced toward the kitchen. She couldn't see out the windows. Branches and leaves blocked her usual view and the odd smell was stronger.

She tapped 911 and went to the front to wait for help. In four minutes that seemed like hours two huge fire trucks came screeching and booming around her corner followed by the fire chief's car and five or six curiosity seekers' cars.

Firemen quickly covered all of her property and ascertained that lightening had hit the beloved old pecan tree causing it to fall and engulf the back of her house. They cut power to a downed line and made sure there was no fire.

"Miss Gillis, this ole tree may have put some holes in your roof. You'll be able to tell better when the crane removes those two big branches. There's no fire though. The smell you mentioned was from the downed lines," the fireman told her.

"How soon do you think the crane can come?" Gert asked knowing it was a weekend and others may need trees removed also.

"You'll be all right a day or so. We reported the damage so you are on their list. Just call them tomorrow and you can get a better idea," he concluded as the firemen prepared to leave.

"Thank you all! Really, thank you, thank you," she called and turned to Fred saying, "Might as well call it a day, ole Buddy. Come."

Fred stayed close by her side as she checked all the doors and windows and went into the den to make sure the fire in the fireplace was out before she climbed the stairs to bed. The storm seemed to have passed and the night sky was beginning to lighten. Water still dripped from the trees but thankfully nothing was dripping indoors.

Halfway up the stairs she paused to catch her breath and thought she might need to change the second parlor into her bedroom. The bath between that room and the kitchen would make it convenient for her when she grew older. Of course she wasn't old yet. Her thoughts turned to this damage as she continued up to bed.

As she undressed in the dark, troubling thoughts raced through her head. Paying for any repairs was her main concern. Social Security covered her basic needs and she had saved the small stipend she received for the literature class she taught at the college for a long anticipated trip to Washington, D.C. Owning an old house wasn't the asset she thought it would be if it needed maintenance. Should she sell and move to a smaller new place? Could she leave these familiar nooks and crannies? She had been offered quite a bit for her property but she couldn't bear the thoughts of strangers living in these rooms, rooms that belonged to her family of ghosts.

"Come, Fred," she called after putting an extra quilt on her bed.

"We won't leave. I'll find a way."

Pass 3

Maude edged her packed SUV into the last space available near the girls' favorite waterfront restaurant. It had been a jubilant jaunt to the curb market in Green Pines as the girls sang like teenagers the words to the songs from the oldies station. Disengaging themselves from plants and pots, food and flowers, Maude helped them pour out onto the sidewalk. Gert remembered seeing Maude do the same with her daughter's softball team earlier in the week.

"This way, ladies," invited a waiter, as he passed the bar heading toward a secluded side area in the noisy colorful waterfront restaurant.

"Oh no, Sonny! We want our usual table right here where the action is," announced Lillian as she plopped her brightly flowered bottom onto a chair at a large round table beside the door to the dock.

14

Tall, slim Penny with nary a wrinkle in skin or linen slid into the chair next to her, saying, "It's a fabulous view of boats hobnobbing in the inlet. "

Stella and Maude were right behind her.

"No wonder this is the favorite restaurant in Green Pines," Gert said apologetically to the waiter, as she took the remaining seat with her back to the dock. She had pushed back the thoughts of her roof scheduled to be inspected Sunday and was determined to enjoy her Saturday. Her motto was "Don't let worry spoil your day."

Maintaining a thin smile the waiter passed menus and was about to take drink orders when a loud noise of a revving motor was followed by the shrieking sound of wood splitting and falling glass. The entire restaurant shook.

A moment of silent shock immobilized witnesses as they watched an overhead sign fall in slow motion onto three tables set for outside dining, scattering glasses, dishes and tableware. An open fisherman had rammed into the dock knocking the piling holding the sign askew. No patrons had been outside so no one seemed to be hurt.

Waiters and a few guests suddenly rushed to the dock edge to help someone obviously in pain being lifted from the boat.

. "Somebody, please call 911," cried the man who had been driving the boat.

A small crowd gathered gaping at the men and the damage. No one reached for their cell phone. The older man seemed to be in as much anguish as the younger one. His eyes met Gertrude's as she nodded and quietly tapped 911.

It wasn't long before an ambulance, the police and the Coast Guard arrived. The injured man was put on his way to the hospital while the driver of the boat was being questioned. Waiters scurried about removing the sign, righting furniture, and sweeping glass and debris. Damage seemed restricted to the dock only so the restaurant remained in operation.

As customers resumed their seats, they could be heard discussing the crash.

"It must have been a rogue wave that hit the boat. The windshield was broken."

"Must have been a big one to knock into the pilot causing him to dislocate his shoulder."

"Heard him say it was his son."

"Same wave shorted out their radio."

"Guess the old geezer will get quite a bill for damage to the dock."

"Wonder why he rammed it."

"Glad no one else was hurt."

Gert noticed Penny jostle the waiter back into reality by resuming the drink orders with, "Make my martini a double." She then put her bouquet of tulips onto a nearby chair.

"Pinot Grigio," Gertrude ordered as she noticed that the handsome driver in the accident had gone.

"Probably gone to check on his friend," she thought, remembering the spark when their eyes met. Had she just imagined it?

While Stella tried to decide between a banana daiquiri and one of the featured drinks with an umbrella, Lillian asked for a rum and coke.

Maude said, "I'm the driver so I'll have my usual sweet tea."

Lillian asked for an extra glass of water for violets she found at the curb market.

"These are sweet violets, like my mother used to have. I hope to find some with roots for my garden." Lillian informed all within earshot.

Gert knew that Lillian was proud that her garden was known as the prettiest one in town. Many of her methods were handed down through families who had lived in the area for hundreds of years. She kept good notes on successes and failures, and histories of the plants as well as uses for them. Herbs from her herb patch by her back door went into most of her cooking, but her specialty was plants used for dye.

"Old Ms. Goings brought me some indigo seeds with instructions on the process to get blue dye. I'd better make a note of that," added Lillian.

Along with the small notebook Lillian pulled from her purse came the card she and Gert had found the night before.

"Whose is this? "Lillian asked.

"Oh, I'll take that," Stella said as she quickly put the card into her pocket offering no explanation to the puzzled faces around her.

"Let's order. I'm starved," she quickly added, putting a stop to any discussion about the card, as she beckoned to the only waiter in sight.

A variety of seafood salads, sandwiches and chowders were soon being served as the girls seemed to forget the boat crash. Their own worries were pushed aside as the conversation turned to the party to be held at the Yacht Club that evening.

"I am expecting all of you to come," Lillian bubbled, "I found enough fresh flowers for each table."

Lillian reveled in being asked to head the hospitality committee Gert noted. She remembered that Lillian's overprotected childhood had left her shy and naive in high school, not too quick in catching onto jokes, often acting as if she felt inferior to her classmates. A typical homebody Lillian raised four daughters and a son, making endless cookies, supporting all the school teams, and tending her garden. Despite her frumpy looks in flowery house dresses, kinky blue hair, and orthopedic shoes, Lillian seemed bright. Gert was glad Lillian had found a job with the local newspaper writing a weekly column of household hints to quell the loneliness of an empty nest. New contacts involved her in new social activities such as the Yacht Club.

"I suppose I have to bring Harold tonight. He wants to be there to see an old sailing buddy who is stopping by until the weather changes. They crewed together when they were boys." Penny said as she rummaged in her purse.

Gert thought of Penny's grumpy husband, Howard, wheelchair bound in their luxurious modern condo on Shell Island. Penny didn't complain often but Gert knew that it was a lot of work for Penny to take him places and meet his many demands. A retired CEO of a large hospital, Howard was used to attention and being in charge.

"Here's my share," Penny added, passing some cash with the newly arrived bill to the others around the table.

As the girls retrieved their belongings, Gert looked at the dock where there was little evidence of the accident that happened only an hour or so earlier. She thought of the father worried about his son. She thought of the man's deep blue eyes.

Pass 4

Before going to the Curb Market Gertrude had called Hank to see when he could come over to inspect her roof for leaks. Hank was a licensed inspector and had been a friend since high school so she felt she could trust his opinion. He told her Sunday morning was the earliest he could come, so she decided to use the free afternoon to browse in Burns' Book Store.

Taking a melon, fresh snap beans, and new potatoes from her canvas tote, she refilled it with several paperbacks she planned to exchange at the bookstore.

Fred insisted on accompanying her, bounding enthusiastically down the block past homes built in the late 1800's facing the waterfront. He barked and she waved at many old friends nearing the center of town passing homes that had added storefronts during the thirties plus a bank and a strip of small cafes and quaint shops geared to tastes of tourists looking for a souvenir of their vacation. She admired these small cinder block stores on Front Street built in the fifties, freshly painted with flowers growing beneath windows that boasted art, antiques, books, ice cream, and a ship's store.

Gone from the waterfront were many of the original New England Colonial and Victorian homes she remembered from her childhood in Seaside, her small hometown. These had been replaced with a hodgepodge of buildings erected since World War II. Additions to the simple buildings bothered her the most. Spanish balconies competed with Colonial porticos and poor copies pretending to be old...

"Flagrant copies create first class Bastard Architecture!" she mumbled to Fred with a vengeance.

She believed in preserving the good examples from the past but new copies she considered architectural plagiarism. She still yearned for a position on the City Planning Board wishing she had gotten her degree in architecture instead of literature.

Ahead, was her favorite old building, once a fish house on the waterfront, now Burns' Bookstore. Her friend, Elizabeth, a fan of the Scottish bard, had run the bookstore for the forty years since she inherited it from her father. She had focused on poetry, the classics, and children's books. A fall made her realize she needed help in the daily management especially during the busy tourist season. She offered the position to her handsome unemployed son who had just graduated from art school. Continuing to work part time Elizabeth gradually gave more responsibilities to him. After computerizing the entire business Bobby's love of art became evident as he began buying good quality art books as well as more contemporary selections. Some of his selections were quite controversial resulting in wide spread attention and greater sales.

Fred settled for a nap under one of the benches that lined the sidewalk in front of the bookstore while Gertrude went inside.

Bobby had the newest fiction displayed in the window as well as a new book on the abstract painter, Rothko. Getting a credit slip for the paperbacks, she made her way toward the art section when she discovered new work by both of her favorite writers from Virginia. Often over the years she had read work by both women at the same time. One wrote with sensitivity of places and times she remembered while the other wrote with wit gently poking fun at old attitudes and customs. Both books went into the canvas bag. The art section of new and used books continued to beckon. Her hunger for books was like a craving. She couldn't understand how anyone could part with some of the old ones she found for sale. Noting with pleasure the color renditions in the new Rothko book she added it to the contents of the bag when some more almost reached out and grabbed her. One was an old copy of Impressionistic *plein aire* paintings done in the wintertime and the other was of modern architects and their work. She stopped browsing, tried to decide what to do. She couldn't afford both. She picked up the book of paintings, put it back and then touched the architecture book, but took neither, thinking that they ought to give gold stars for resisting temptation.

As she turned to get in the line by the register someone behind her said, "Pardon me, aren't you the young lady who dialed 911 for my son at the Restaurant on the Pier earlier today?"

She could barely answer, "Why, yes," as she recognized him and felt that spark again as she looked into his deep blue eyes.

"I am so glad to find you so I can say 'thank you'. As soon as the police would let me leave, I rushed to the hospital to check on my son."

"How is your son? I hope he wasn't hurt badly."

"They have set his dislocated shoulder so he is resting now. I came here to get him something to read while he convalesces."

As her books were being rung up, she noted his stack of paperbacks adding, "I notice he must like sea stories."

"A couple are for me," he laughed, catching up as they went out the door.

"My name is Harris Graham, by the way."

"Gertrude Gillis," she said and smiled as they shook hands with Fred coming close to stand between them.

"Well, I need to get back to the hospital now, but I hope to see you again."

She smiled her answer, adding, "I hope your son is better soon," as they parted.

Walking home the sun seemed warmer as she thought of those deep blue eyes. They were as warm and strong as his hand shake. She wondered who he was, why he was here on his son's boat out in such windy weather, and why was he going so fast coming into a dock.

By the time she reached home the bag of books was growing heavy and she looked forward to a cup of tea and a good long reading session. As soon as she opened the door, she heard the phone ringing. It was Stella.

"Stell, I can't understand what you are saying. Just hang in there. Don't cry. I'll be right over."

In less than ten minutes, Stella opened her door a crack and invited Gert in. It was dark in the living room with the shades drawn against the sunny day.

Stella eyes were running over as she whispered to Gertrude, "Oh, Gert, I have a lump in my breast and I am so scared."

"So that was your appointment card Lillian found? What did the doctor say?"

"I never went to the doctor's office. I was too scared!"

"Oh. Stell, why didn't you tell us? That's what friends are for. If you will call and reschedule, I'll go with you. The sooner you do something about it the sooner you'll be better."

"I really don't want to hear bad news."

"It may be nothing and you are worrying for nothing, or if it is something, the earlier it is detected, the easier it is to deal with it."

"Okay, I'll call," she reluctantly promised. Gert watched as she dialed and set up a new appointment for late the following Tuesday afternoon.

"Now let's plan on going to the Yacht Club party! Whatcha gonna' wear?" Gert asked, hoping to get Stella's mind on something cheerful.

Watching Stella select dresses from her closet promising to join the rest at the party that evening, Gert thought, "In high school I was so jealous of Stella! She had big boobs and all the boys liked her best. Then she got in trouble and ran off with Hector. What a drunk he became! I wonder whatever happened to him. Stella doesn't know if she is married or not! She had a son, Dennis, I think. I wonder where he is now."

When Gertrude started to leave Stella said, "Now Gert, promise you won't tell. I don't want everybody fussing over me. I know it's silly but I always felt that I had done something very wrong when I got sick, I don't want everybody blaming me or feeling sorry for me."

"That is probably due to the way we all treated her when she got PG in high school," Gertrude thought to herself but said, "I'll promise if you promise to be at the party."

Gertrude didn't really want to go out again that evening, but she had promised Stella, so she drove home to get ready. She decided it was better to focus on cheering Stella than to sit at home brooding about Hank's inspection tomorrow.

Pass 5

"I'm coming!" Stella called out when Gert approached her door, while Lillian waited in the car to drive them to an evening at the Yacht Club.

"I'll be with you as soon as I find my keys!" she added, as she put her large straw carryall out on the porch. Her porch looked like a yard sale gone awry. Every table and chair was full, holding anything from flowers in pots to whirligigs, baskets and rocks. Macramé designs and wind chimes made of seashells, clay, metal and wood hung overhead. Even the trees in the yard seemed over decorated with wisteria vines beginning to bloom hanging from every branch. It was a slightly run down Victorian house, a shabby aristocrat on a street of yesterdays.

Three handsome cats, one obviously very pregnant, came running as Stella reappeared, this time with a bowl of cat food. She poured water into another bowl.

"I'm coming," she apologized, "As soon as I find my new blue scarf."

She disappeared back into the house leaving the door ajar.

Through the door Gert could smell cat pee of which Stella was totally unaware. She could see colorful lengths of cloth, ready to be used in Stella's next project, piled on the sofa. Four more cats pounced and played as Stella rummaged through the cloth looking for the lost scarf.

"This will do," Stella said, as she wrapped a magenta silk scarf around her coppery hair and pulled a fuzzy white jacket over her blue leather mini skirt.

"I'm coming," she smiled at Gert's raised eyebrows, "As soon as I find my ear rings."

Gert tried not to show her disapproval of Stella dressing as a teenager. Stella had never admitted to being as old as the other three, even refusing senior citizen discounts. Gert figured that subconsciously Stella really didn't want to attend tonight's party.

From a branch of the dancing palm tree that twisted to the sound waves from the radio, Stella selected a pair of ear rings, turned off the radio and checked in the mirror for another wrinkle.

"Darn those face-lifts. They don't stay lifted," Gert heard her mumble as she finally emerged and struggled to lock her door.

Gert gave Stella a reassuring pat as they joined Lillian for their short drive to Shell Island. Nearing the bridge traffic had come to a stop as the draw was open to let shrimp boats pass. Lillian opened the windows to enjoy the familiar view as the sturdy work boats plowed toward home docks. Their outriggers swayed while green nets hanging out to dry glistened in the late afternoon sun. The tangy smell of shrimp and low tide floated in on the salty breeze.

"That's the smell of good luck!" exclaimed Stella, as she crossed her fingers thinking of her pending appointment. They agreed.

Arriving at the yacht club early, Lillian checked pots of early blooming tulips and daffodils, decorations she had put on the tables earlier, then the girls joined other early arrivals sitting near the bar in the Tiki hut set up at the end of the dock.

Accepting tall glasses of iced tea laced with rum, they listened to the ongoing conversation about plans for the summer pram fleet. All of the prams had been repaired and were ready but they hadn't yet found anyone willing to be the instructor. Gert knew it was one of the projects dear to Lillian's heart as her husband, Harold, had been their first instructor. Just as Lill began to reminisce about those early days when the seasoned sailors taught the young members to sail the dinner bell rang.

This was spaghetti night and the Chef was ready to take orders for ingredients in each serving of sauce as people came through the buffet line.

Penny and Howard had not yet arrived. It was a lovely evening with good food, and old friends stopping by their table to say hello. A local band set up between the bar and the dessert table and began to play mellow swing from the forties and fifties. A wood fire was lit to offset the chill following sunset.

Lillian whispered to Gert that Stella was not her usual talkative self and that she was drinking more than usual, when Stella began quietly sobbing. With a questioning look on her face Lillian went along as Gertrude led Stella to the Ladies Room.

"Stella, dear, don't cry. What's the matter?" Lillian began.

"I'm sorry. I'm so scared. I might have, you know, the C word. I can't say it. I have a lump," Stella cried.

Hugs and tissues were passed around as Stella continued to sob.

"Remember I'll be with you Tuesday when you see Dr. Gibson," Gert reminded her.

"I feel so old," Stella wailed.

"Well, you're not," reprimanded Gert. "We're all the same age and we will stick together and everything will be fine. You just wait and see!"

"Oh, girls, if it weren't for you all, I'd be all alone. My son is lost to me. I miss him so. I need to find him before I die so I can tell him I love him,"

"And it's my fault," Stella added with a far away look.

"You had no choice, Stell. When Hector ran off it must have been tough raising a teenage boy alone. When he got into drugs, what else could you do but tell him quit or get out?" Gert said.

"It's not your fault, "agreed Lillian "So dry your eyes and lets go back."

On the way back to their table Gert leaned close to Stella and whispered, "When we were kids you wanted to be an actress. Well, this is your big chance. Pretend to enjoy the evening, even if it kills you. "

The band was taking a break and announcements were being made as they returned to their table. Penny and Howard's absence was noticeable when Howard's sailing buddy was introduced by the Commodore as a notable past member.

They ordered dessert for all and coffee for Stella when the band began to play "Smoke Gets in Your Eyes." Harris Graham, handsome in a camel jacket and dark slacks stopped at their table. Recognizing him from earlier Lillian and Stella stared while Gertrude introduced him.

"Good evening ladies. I hope you don't mind if I ask Trudy to dance," he smiled, bowing gallantly.

Gert glanced at Stella and Lillian. Both nodded, "Go ahead."

As he swept her across the dance floor, she could see them watching with open mouth expressions probably wondering who he was and when had she met him. Did they notice he had called her Trudie, with affectionate familiarity of an old friend?

She felt she was floating as Harris led her around the room. She was not aware of others dancing nearby. She forgot her troubles and Stella's worries. She didn't talk, only thought of his touch, his smell, and the way he made her feel all tingly and excited inside.

The band was now playing another song and another.

By the time they returned to the table Lillian said Stella was ready to go home. Before Gert could comment, Harris said, "Please, let me take you home." Gertrude consented to Harris' offer so it was with raised eyebrows that the girls told her good night.

Pass 6

Gertrude was enjoying a second cup of coffee while reading the Sunday paper on her sunny side porch as she waited for Hank to finish inspecting her roof, when the phone rang.

"Gert, this is Lillian. I just talked to Penny and we have to do something! Howard is livid! He found out that Phyllis is bringing a guest when she comes home next weekend. He says he won't have it. He is yelling and cursing again this morning. Penny says that's why they didn't come to the party last night. Howard can be so abusive! He never hits her but his verbal abuse is devastating. She never says a word back to him, She's afraid of him, I guess."

"I can't leave now. The city crane just left. They lifted the branches off my roof and now Hank is up there assessing the damage."

"I'll try to think of something," Gert continued. "If you go over there, tell Penny that we will help somehow. You know how independent she is. She pretends all is okay while she looks for her solution with another martini."

"Stella and I are going to see the new art exhibit in town this afternoon. Maybe we can get Penny to go with us," replied Lillian. "Join us if you can."

Just as she hung up Hank joined her bringing another mug and the coffee pot from the kitchen. Refilling her mug and his, he sat down and helped himself to a muffin before beginning.

"Well Gert, I know you want the truth. Even the patches need patching but I wouldn't advise it. You need a new roof. I've worked with HARB before and in this historic district they will insist on replacing your shingle roof with wooden shingles again. I'm afraid it will be pretty expensive."

"Oh," was all she could say thinking of her limited funds.

"My suggestion would be to talk to HARB. They may have a solution."

"Thanks, Hank. I guess I have a few decisions to make," she added as Hank rose to go.

After Hank left, she continued to sit there thinking of her beloved old Victorian house where she had lived all of her life. After her high school sweetheart had died in the war, it was here she found solace and protection. Here the book lined walls were a comfort. Here she could touch a banister worn by family hands over the years, or look out the same kitchen window as her mother had, or share a view of the garden as she had with her father. Did she need all these rooms? Weren't they extra work, waxing, polishing, and painting? If she sold the house, she could afford a modern minimalist condo in the city with museums and work nearby. It was just too much to think about this morning she decided.

Hoping to turn off the ricocheting thoughts, she went inside and sat down to practice the piano. She was not a musician but it was a comfort to play her great grandmother's upright piano.

"Scales first," she could almost hear her mother say.

After warming her fingers on a few scales, she turned to her old sheet music playing songs from the time when there were no problems greater than what to wear to a dance.

Looking at her watch as the doorbell broke her reverie, she realized it was nearly one in the afternoon and she was hungry.

"Harris!" she said, when she opened the door. "I'm so surprised to see you."

"Please forgive me for not calling first. My cell phone went overboard when I was in the boat and I haven't replaced it yet. I'm on my way back to the hospital and I wanted to bring you this," he said as he handed her a book.

"Do come in. I'm getting ready to fix some lunch. Won't you join me?" she smiled.

"I'd love too. I'm starving!"

"And thank you," she added as she led him back toward the kitchen. "This is the book about modern architects I admired in the bookstore yesterday. How did you know? How did you get it? They don't open on Sundays."

"I noticed you in the book store. I noticed that you have a love for books as I do. This book came from my collection. I brought a few of my favorites with me when I came down even though my apartment is only temporary."

As she took out bread, tomatoes, lettuce, cheese, and thin slices of ham, he offered to help and began cutting the bread for sandwiches as she put water on for tea.

It was a pleasant lunch with sunlight streaming into the old-fashioned kitchen where they sat on stools pulled up to the butcher block work table.

Fred was lying beside the back door watching workmen clear the yard of the last branches blown down by the storm.

Conversation focused on their mutual love of modern architecture. Both agreed upon the importance of preserving structures as art that reflected past periods. Both were delighted to discover that they also agreed that art and architecture of the present should reflect the present!

Harris leafed through the book of architecture showing her some of his favorites. It seemed they were old friends as they shared memories of favorite buildings in other cities.

Gertrude told him about how she was looking forward to a summer of reading with a possible trip to D.C. Since being at the University her personal reading had been put on hold as her schedule was busy teaching eighteenth century literature as well as freshman creative writing.

"I've been saving for a trip to DC all year but it may have to be postponed," she sighed, "Since HARB, the Historical Architectural Restoration Board, may insist that I replace my roof with expensive wooden shingles, but what can I say, after all I am in favor of authenticity."

"Talk to them on the board. They may know of a solution," he advised.

He told her that he had rented an apartment for the summer season. He had recently retired as a journalist for a major newspaper in Washington, D.C. and was looking forward to a quiet summer for reading and writing.

"My son and I were out on the water inspecting some property Saturday between Green Pines and Shell Island and had just decided to check out Seaside also when the weather suddenly changed," he explained when she expressed concern.

"We were in the roughest part of the inlet east of Shell Island when a large wave came straight on causing us to flounder. Then a second wave crashed into the cabin, breaking glass, shorting out the radio and knocking Dean, onto the deck. I steered the best I could to the nearest dock for help."

"At the dock I tried to put it into reverse," he related shaking his head, "It didn't go into reverse."

As she sliced a chilled melon for dessert, he repeated, "It didn't go into reverse. "

When she offered to make some Irish coffee Harris declined, saying, "I need to get back to the hospital. My son and his doctor may make a decision today about surgery on his shoulder. I want to be there to lend support."

"I'm falling for this guy!" she thought to herself as they parted with his promise to call later.

Pass 7

It was a glorious fresh Monday morning with gulls laughing and scolding overhead as Gert and Stella walked past the marina approaching Penny's condominium. Freshly washed and polished ocean going sailboats vied for attention side by side in their berths. Various flags fluttered in the breeze.

"There's one from Ireland," pointed Stella, "and another from Great Britain."

"I wonder where they're going," commented Gert as they watched a young couple load duffle bags onto a sleek trimaran near the condo entrance.

"I'd never be bored living here," Stella smiled as they entered the elevator from the condo lobby.

"It's working," Gert thought to herself, "I got her to smile."

Penny greeted them saying, "Come in. I'm almost ready. Maybe you would enjoy the view from the balcony while I make sure Howard is taken care of. "

There was a stiff breeze blowing from the inlet as the girls stepped out onto the third story balcony but the girls didn't mind. The view here where Shell Island was only four miles wide, was fantastic.

"Look! There's the draw to Sea Side, Gert," Stella exclaimed excitedly, "And today I can see all the way to the banks offshore."

"Those early sea captains knew a safe place to build their homes," answered Gert thinking of the Seaside townhouses built in the 1800's.

"I can almost see Lillian's neighborhood too," Stella said looking toward Green Pines on her far right.

Morning sunlight streaming into the condo from the balcony, created cozy seclusion high above the traffic of working boats trudging through the inlet past the marina to fish houses farther inland.

Gert could hear Penny say, "Howard, here's the Times and the Journal. The doorman just brought them up. There's freshly brewed coffee and hot muffins on the breakfront. May I get you anything else before I leave?"

"Humph," grunted a gray haired immaculately groomed old gentlemen as he wheeled himself toward the breakfront.

"The once powerful CEO of a network of hospitals doesn't like the dependency brought on by a recent stroke," thought Gert.

Penelope placed a crystal compote of orange marmalade near the edge of the silver tray so her grumpy husband could reach it.

With a quick glance Gert noticed that the room was neat as a pin. She knew Penny was proud of the oasis she had created with Howard's family's English antiques and her family's paintings. A few carefully selected pieces, a sterling teapot or a cloisonné vase, rotated with the seasons, adorned the highly polished mahogany surfaces. Muted colored Persian rugs on the smooth wooden floor defined areas of activity in the large open expanse. Comfortable leather chairs with Sheraton side tables made conversational grouping near the modern black marble fireplace.

"I just love Penny's place," Stella purred, "She deserves pretty things. Remember how she would always share in the fifth grade?"

"Yes, I do," agreed Gert. "And she still shares."

Gert believed that the oasis of refinement Penny created for her retirement as the wife of a renowned philanthropist brought her pleasure and satisfaction. Having attended exclusive girls' schools, she seemed to lead a prim and proper lifestyle as a leader in urban society. She sat on many prestigious boards, chaired many openings, traveled extensively in Europe and now acted ready for quiet times with old friends. She no longer had a social secretary. Dinner guests could now be seated at her table for eight.

"I'm glad you are going with us to Lillian's," Stella said as Penny ushered them out and into the elevator.

"Even for an informal event," Gert noted. "Penny wears an Italian leather jacket over an old white blouse and brown linen slacks."

She saw Penny smooth her dark hair and check her slim silhouette in the elevator's full length mirror. No jewelry was added to the diamonds dripping from her fingers and ears.

Gert thought of the old saying, "You can never be too thin or too rich."

As they piled into Gert's old car she turned the radio to the oldies station, saying, "Which floor, ladies?"teasing them about their choice of elevator music but she too knew the words to their favorites. Laughing and singing they were soon on their way west to Lillian's home in Green Pines.

When they arrived, Gert had a touch of deja vu. She wondered how many times she had stopped in front of this house where Lillian and Harold had raised their five children. Harold made a comfortable living from his store a couple of blocks away and their home was always open to friends of any age. After Gert's high school sweetheart was killed in the war it would have been a lonely life with only an occasional dinner date but Lillian and Harold always included her in their parties and gatherings. Lillian had no sister so Gert had become the favorite aunt, sharing good times and bad, with the family. When Harold died Gert was the one the children asked for advice about helping their mother. Gert knew what it was to be lonely. Work had been her answer.

The motor was barely off when Lillian and several grandchildren rushed out to welcome them and invite them inside. The house smelled of fresh air, lemon oil and soap. Gert figured Lillian had spent all morning cleaning and polishing with all the windows open.

"Are you really going to make blue dye, Lill?" asked Penny handing her an armful of folded white cloth. "These are the softest sheets I could find."

"Yes. We'll dye in the back yard. The kids are stringing extra clothes lines," Lillian answered as she took the cloth. "Thanks. These are for batik!"

"I have all your notes about medicinal plants typed and organized right here," added Gert holding up a small disk.

"Wow, thank you," Lillian smiled. "I always loved gardening. I never dreamed it would come to a column about plants. Your encouragement did it," Lillian went on.

"You won all their awards. " Stella boasted with pride.

"You shared your plants and knowledge with all of your neighbors. No wonder they responded with stories of plants told to them by the past generation," added Penny.

"People will love a weekly column about plants," Gert told her thinking it was good for Lillian's self image to get accolades for her work. Lillian had once told her how she felt inferior having not been to college. Lill said she chose to stay home and raise five kids and wouldn't have changed that for the world but when they grew up and moved away she was dreadfully lonely, so gardening was her only recreation. Gert had seen the detailed notes Lillian made and volunteered to organize them which led to the column.

"It was easy," said Gert. "Now I'm ready to do the ones used for natural dyes."

"Thanks, I'm still working on them," Lillian replied. "Let's see what Stella brought."

They all gathered around while Stella covered the table with delicate line drawings of plants. Some had roots, some blossoms, all done in ink with a coquille pen that made thick and thin lines.

The girls looked at Stella in stunned silence.

"Oh, Stella, they are exquisite."

"God, they're so beautiful."

"I didn't know you could do this,"

Stella simply said, "Thanks," as her eyes overflowed with happiness.

Assorted grand children came in from the back announcing that the fire was ready for Grandma's magic. Lillian laughed and picked up an old roaster pan filled with potting soil.

"Indigo seeds are in here," she said to one of the children. "When they sprout, you can plant the seedlings under the walnut tree where there is both sun and shade."

"The old walnuts, hulls and all," Lillian explained, "will make a rich brown dye for the last baskets I made of purchased reeds. My honeysuckle and grape vine baskets look best in their natural state. The brown walnut dye will also be a nice contrast for the batik I'm going to do on that unbleached cloth I just found."

Lillian's daughter Maude greeted the girls and let her mother take over stirring the big iron pot of boiling fermented indigo plants.

"Yeew, Yuck" was heard midst giggles and disgusted faces.

"The children heard old Miss Goings tell Ma to save a chamber pot of pee for this process." Maude informed the girls.

"It wasn't easy to do that with a house full of grandchildren so she found the chemical equivalent," she added

All eyes were on Lillian as she added the smelly liquid to the big iron pot boiling over a fire in the backyard.

Adding skeins of hand spun yarn she allowed each child to stir the pot with a large wooden spoon while saying the magic words, "Boil and bubble, Toil and trouble, if good and true, turn to blue."

Carefully she helped each child take wet dripping yarn out of the pot, draping it over the lines tied from tree to tree in the shade.

. They were astounded as the yarn gradually turned blue while it oxidized in the air. The girls were surprised also.

"The yarn will get repeated washing and rinsing," Lillian explained, "And be stored with dried lavender. I plan to knit blue mufflers for each grandchild here today."

"With new interests and attention Lillian no longer seems worried about growing old," Gert thought with a sigh of relief as they were leaving.

"What about Penny and Stella?" she pondered after dropping them off, "How will they cope? Penny's husband is getting harder to manage and poor Stell may be very ill."

Rounding the corner to her street she could see the blue tarp on her roof, reminding her of her own worries. Images of a roof shingled with hundred dollar bills ran through her mind and her as a rag-a-muffin standing in front battling HARB with her mop and pail.

Pass 8

Gertrude finished setting up the card table and chairs on her sunny porch. She could hardly believe it was her turn to host the Friday afternoon bridge game. It had been an eventful busy week.

Late Tuesday afternoon during a heavy rainfall she had accompanied Stella to what would probably be many appointments. After a surprisingly short consultation a stoic Stella rejoined her with a schedule for a battery of tests clutched in her hand. Knowing Stella's reluctance to keep appointments, Gert called on Lillian and Penny for encouragement and help accompanying her to each.

Grading mid term exams and student essays had filled her evenings leaving no time to be with her friends or to accept Harris' invitations to dinner. She hoped to finish grading papers leaving her free the following week to enjoy Spring Break and perhaps to spend some time with Harris. She was anxious to hear of Stella's diagnosis and of Penny's situation.

Someone knocked "Shave and a Haircut" as the front door opened with laughter and voices of her best friends preceded them coming through the house. Penny and Stella were pushing Lillian in front saying, "Tell her!"

"It's so exciting!"

"Wait until you hear!"

"Our own Lillian is going to be famous!"

"Oh hush now," Lillian said as she handed Gert a bunch of fresh mint.

"They haven't made an offer yet. They haven't even read all of the notes yet."

"Thank you Lill, I'll put some in our tea and plant the rest as you recommended under that spigot that drips," Gert said, leading the girls to the porch.

"Now tell me your news!"

"Maude told one of her friends about the notes I've kept on my plants," Lillian began.

"And after he read some of my notes and three columns he suggested a book of plants of eastern Carolina. He seemed most interested in the notes on their history."

"He hasn't read about your dye garden yet" added Penny as she spread cards on the table and drew one.

"Don't forget to show him our wildflower collection, too," put in Stella, as she and the others drew a card.

"Yes, Lill, you identified all of the photos and drawings you and Stella collected over the past summers."

"Stella's sensitive line drawings will sell the book," beamed Lillian.

"Lillian's vast knowledge on medicinal plants is extraordinary," Stella added.

"Gert lent her talents as editor. Shall I be your sales manager?" asked Penny.

"Yeah," rang the chorus

Gert compared the drawn cards saying, "It's your deal, Lillian."

Lillian looked at her hand quietly, then blurted, "Have you heard from your tests yet, Stella? One heart."

"No! Pass," answered Stella crossly volunteering no information.

"One spade. I hope all of you are going to the Chamber's Pig Pickin' tomorrow night," was Gert's attempt to change the subject.

They all knew a Pig Pickin' was the favorite method of feeding a large celebratory crowd in their community

"I hope the weather is nice since they are holding it on the bluff east of town. Two diamonds," bid Penny. "State dignitaries are expected as well as all the local politicians"

"I hope it is nice weather since they've asked Howard to introduce the architect whose designs will be used for the development. Two spades," bid Lillian.

"I saw a model of the houses in it - very modern! Pass."

"Finally a breath of fresh air in this old town. Three hearts."

"But it will look so-o different - won't fit in at all. Pass."

"This is the first big change in a long time. A lot is riding on it. Four hearts."

"Pass." "Pass." "Pass."

Stella led with the Jack of diamonds to Gert's dummy which had only a pair of diamonds. Lillian wondered if Stella remembered the rule to lead your highest card in your partner's suit. She let it ride forcing Penny's King. Penny gathered all trumps from Stella and Lillian before leading to the hearts on the board, lost one diamond and one club trick, trumping the remaining tricks.

Over the years the hostess was always partner to the first dealer. First dealer always kept score. This gave the hostess time to attend to luncheon preparations between hands. At the end of two rubbers the table was cleared and Gert spread it with one of her cut work bridge cloths that had belonged to her mother. She used her grandmother's sterling silver flatware and Haviland china to serve pineapple/shrimp salad plus tender asparagus and steamed baby carrots. The girls appreciated the lovely presentation as much as the sparkling white wine that was Gert's favorite.

Plans for the coming week were discussed as the girls enjoyed lunch with Penelope saying, "Phyllis still isn't sure when she will arrive. She says it depends on the weather! And she alludes to a big surprise. Thanks Gert, for offering your spare room. I'll let you know if and when I hear more."

"Heavens that child always has been a free spirit," laughed Lillian. "Has Howard simmered down now that he knows they won't be staying with you?"

"My daughter will always be welcome to stay with me. It's her friends who are the problem."

"At least you hear from her and about all her exploits, wild as they are," put in Stella, as the girls exchanged knowing looks.

No one spoke of Stella being lonely for her distant son Dennis but they made her promise to let them know of her test results as soon as she heard. She had to agree for she couldn't hide from them. It was her turn to have the game at her place next week. As they discussed this and the Pig Pickin', Gert brought out dessert.

"Oh, Gert, it is so pretty," was Penelope's rare compliment.

"Thinking of your daughter reminded me of it. She liked to make it when she was little and would visit me when you and Howard were out of town."

"I remember Jell-O pie! We all used to make it back in the fifties," smiled Lillian, adding, "And it tastes so good!"

"I don't remember it. I was too young. I was chasing boys back then," Stella quipped. "Tell me how to make it."

"Just melt a pint of vanilla ice cream in hot Jell-O. Then add a can of drained fruit cocktail and pour into a pie pan lined with vanilla wafers and chill," Gertrude answered.

"Too young?"

"We were all in the same class!"

With hugs all around as the girls were leaving, Gert said, "Oh I forgot to tell you - I asked Harris to go with me to the Pig Pickin'." Whoops and giggles spouted from four old ladies acting like teenagers.

"Tell us about him!"

"Have you been out with him?"

"What's he like?"

The three old friends all turned eager to hear all about a possible new man in their midst and waited for Gert to continue.

"He's a retired journalist and he and his son were looking at waterfront property the day he bumped into the restaurant in Green Pines. He found out, by the way, that the nut on the gear cable housing was loose which prevented it from going into reverse that day."

"No, I mean what is he like, quiet? funny? sexy?"

"What does he like, sports? poetry? fishing?"

"What's it like with him, fun? exciting? safe?"

"Wait, wait, wait. You'll meet him tomorrow night," said Gert, shooing them away.

Pass 9

The late sun cast long shadows on the ground beneath the huge old oak trees as Gertrude and Harris approached the bluff. A tantalizing aroma of roast pork welcomed them as soon as they drove up in his little green Miata.

Men from the Chamber who had been tending the fire all day and the preceding night could be heard joking and greeting the arriving guests. It was a chore traditionally accompanied with whisky and many tall tales.

Harris was captivated by the view from the bluff of the inland waterway and the islands offshore. A few wild ponies could be seen grazing on the island to the south with the light house in the distance. The local pram fleet was taking their last lap around the sand bar to the east before sundown.

"Reminds me of the days when Dean learned to sail," said Harris. He gave Gertrude a tight squeeze as they stood for a few silent minutes before following others down to the beach below.

Picnic tables placed near the fire pit held platters of hush puppies, slaw, baked beans, corn on the cob, and steaming bowls of collards. Coolers of beer and soft drinks were scattered about among the picnic tables where happy hour was in full swing. On the left near the bluff a band was setting up on a temporary stage made of plywood over metal drums. Closer to the water a bon fire was being readied.

Greeting friends as they made their way toward the crowd, they saw Stella and Lillian waving them over to their table. Since Stella's doctor confirmed that her lump was cancerous Lillian had not left her side.

A stoic Penelope was standing by an impatient Howard in his wheelchair.

As introductions were made Howard asked, "Are you the Harris Dean Graham who designed this development? At the last minute we were told he could not be present tonight."

All eyes turned toward Harris as he answered, "That's my son, Dean. He is in the hospital due to a boating accident. He wanted to come but the doctors said 'No'."

Wishes for his son's speedy recovery were heard all around as well as congratulations. Most had seen the architectural models in the bank. Looking at Gert's open mouth stare Harris added, "I planned to tell you tonight. There's more. He will have surgery tomorrow. I will move into his apartment to help him for a few weeks until he can manage on his own."

Gert was about to mention her week free of classes when she saw the total shock on Howard and Penelope's faces.

Turning she heard, "Mother! Daddy!" and looking like a beautiful gypsy with black hair flying was Phyllis running toward her parents.

"We made it - just in time. I love you!" beamed Phyllis.

Hugs, kisses and smiles hesitated as Howard said, "We?"

Bursting with excitement Phyllis pulled a tall lanky fellow carrying a bass fiddle over to meet them. "This is my handsome husband, Gordon!"

"Husband?" The entire crowd seemed to stop breathing at once.

"We sailed the last leg of our journey on the outside in the Gulf stream so we made good time. We got here a day early. I tried to call you as we came into port but you had already left. Meanwhile, one of Gordo's friends asked him to fill in for this shindig."

With polite handshakes, a kiss on top of Phyllis's head and, "Gotta' run, Babe. Excuse me, folks," Gordon joined the band on stage.

Announcements were made about the new development. A shaken Howard explained about Dean Graham's absence. Guests were invited to celebrate with food and drinks and the band began to play as folks lined up to get barbequed pork and "the fixings."

Phyllis could be heard explaining to her mother that she and Gordon, a professional musician, were on their honeymoon and thanks, but they planned to stay on their sailboat.

The girls exchanged looks of excitement, pride, pleasure and friendship as the lighthouse beamed over the first beach party of the season.

Pass 10

Gert folded the card again, slipped it under the wobbly table leg and unpacked cards, pencils, score pads, a bag of mints and four bottles of peach tea. Penny put a cooler nearby and helped pull chairs into place. They were about to comment on how dreary it was in the quiet rehab room when Lillian came through the door pushing an ashen Stella in a wheel chair right up to the card table.

"You're looking well, Stella," lied Penny as she dealt the cards.

"The surgery went well," volunteered Stella "And will be followed by radiation, some new drugs and no chemo."

"A few days in rehab will help you gather strength before returning home," added Gert. "Then you'll feel better," she smiled.

Gert knew Stella had several days of deep depression, feeling very old and undesirable.

Big smiles and huge hugs were shared, cards were dealt, and the bidding had begun, when Stella said, "This is the nicest gift you could have given me. I feel I am getting back to normal again. Three clubs!"

Three No Trump was her partner's bid leaving Stella as dummy, which was an advantage as reaching out to play the cards was still difficult for her to do. As she watched the girls play, the feeling of self pity seemed to leave her. She could hardly wait to be at home again, back to reality.

The next hand brought four passes so the girls decided to postpone the game and see what hostess Penny had brought in her cooler.

"Wait," said Lillian as she gathered the cards, unfolded a fringed Indian Head cloth and four matching napkins, paper plates and plastic tableware.

Penny managed to serve warm chicken tenders, cool cold slaw, and potato salad plus elegant croissants. Gert added a surprise bouquet of flowers to the center of the table. It was a delightful supper, a cheerful respite to Stella's day.

"We haven't missed many weekly get togethers. Thanks girls," Stella said as she waved to the person pushing a small cart down the hall.

"It was my turn as hostess so let me at least furnish dessert, "she offered and ice cream cones were served to all.

As they sat as children quietly licking ice cream, Penny turned to Stella and asked. "Would you mind if my computer whiz daughter tried to find Dennis?"

"Oh, do you think she could? Oh, yes. Please ask her to try."

Looking for Dennis is already Stella's best possible prescription Gert thought as she watched Stella give Penny basic facts to use in the search.

"Speaking of computers, my editor has all of your drawings on the computer set in place with the script. He hopes to get one more from you for the cover," Lillian said, wiping ice cream from her chin.

Gert was happy to see Stella's spirits high as plans were made for next week's game before they packed to leave.

African Blue Basil

Jean

Pass 11

The sweet aroma of Cape jasmine permeated the cool interior of Penny's condo filling Gert with nostalgia. It was the epitome of a June day on the coast.

Arriving a little early for bridge she joined Penny and Phyllis pouring over a site on Penny's computer.

"I think this is the one," Phyllis exclaimed excitedly as she printed a page. "Show Stella and maybe she would like to call him."

"Dad's waiting downstairs for me to give him a ride to his meeting on my way to the beach," she added blowing kisses as she gathered towels, an umbrella, two books and a bag of chips and flew out the door.

"I sure hope that's Stella's son. Phyllis is a terrific girl, Penny."

"She has Howard wrapped around her little finger again. Last night she got him out to have drinks at the club where her husband, Gordy, is playing now."

"Today she made it easier for me to have our game here," smiled Penny as she turned from the computer.

"While we're alone, Gert," Penny began, "I want you to know I will be happy to help you with your roof. I know how independent you are. We could call it a loan."

"What a wonderful friend you are," Gert expressed emotionally, "Thank you, I think I have found a solution."

Gert was about to continue when Lillian and Stella arrived. Penny served mimosas as a prelude to the weekly bridge game.

Lillian stopped shuffling cards as Penny gave Stella a paper saying, "This may be your son, Stella."

A look of wonder was on Stella's face as she reached out very gently to touch the photograph on the page whispering, "Dennis?"

No one moved to play cards. Each filled with compassion, silently clasped Stella's hand until Penny's oven timer broke the spell.

"The quiche is ready," Penny announced going into the kitchen.

"Let's eat it then," suggested Lillian and she put away the cards and brought over the cut work cloth and napkins she spied waiting on a nearby table.

Gert knew where Penny kept her silver and quietly finished setting the table.

Penny served cool fruit salad with warm quiche making a colorful and delicious luncheon especially with additional mimosas.

Stella was the one to change the subject brightly asking Gert, "How did your meeting go with big bad buddies on the HARB board? Do they still sit on stage looking down at you as you speak into the microphone?"

"Yes," laughed Gert. "But I was determined not to let them know I was nervous. They really aren't so bad. They insisted on wooden shingles, but made a surprising suggestion."

All eyes were on Gert as she continued. "A national paint company is looking for an old house to restore and use in their national advertising campaign. The board would like for me to agree because it would be good exposure for Sea Side as well."

"What did you decide?"

"When would they do it?"

"Would you have to move out while the work is being done?"

"Yes, I agreed. Signed the papers yesterday with the stipulation that I move out and that they can start as soon as school is out."

"You may stay with me," Lillian volunteered.

"Or me," added Stella.

"It sounds like a good decision," commented Penny.

"The good part is, now I can afford a new roof and go to DC like I'd planned if someone will just feed Fred and check on things occasionally," Gert put in hopefully.

"A few bridge games will be postponed but we will all check," promised Penny.

"We'll be busy but we'll miss you," Stella whispered with Dennis' picture still clutched in her left hand.

"I'll feed Fred but what about Harris?" teased Lillian, "He'll miss you too."

"No, he won't. He's going with me."

Pass 12

Gertrude dressed quickly in white jeans and a new red silk blouse as Harris waited to take her to the opening of Sea Bluff, a cluster of contemporary townhouses, designed by his son Dean. She knew Harris was quite proud of his son's achievements. So much had happened since the initial ground breaking back in the spring. Dean's surgery had gone well and it wasn't long before he was back at work. It was the first major construction Dean had designed and was hailed as 'a breath of fresh air' in the conservative seacoast area.

When Dean had his boat repaired, it was discovered that the nut on the shift cable had been loosened so it didn't go into reverse when you shifted gears. This discovery relieved Harris from blame for ramming the dock. Dean's insurance covered the damages. Since then, Gert had enjoyed sharing excursions on the water with them on weekends.

When Harris moved back to his apartment, he had a chance to show off his talents as a gourmet chef. Quite often he would call her when she got home from school saying, "Trudie, you've gotta come over and taste this."

She introduced him to little known spots in the neighborhood such as the goat trails under the yaupon trees, or the remains of an old forgotten lighthouse on the outer banks.

It had been a busy end of the year teaching plus term papers to grade while preparing to leave her house unattended while out of town.

Harris volunteered to be her tour guide in his old neighborhood, D.C. The quick trip lengthened into three months as they stayed in his family home in Georgetown and leisurely explored art galleries, attended concerts and were entertained by his friends.

"You look gorgeous!" Harris exclaimed as he kissed her neck and turning to Fred added, "Take care of things, ole boy. We won't be gone long this time."

Fred was so glad to see Gert when she returned that he didn't seem to mind that Harris had moved in with her, no longer standing between them. Lillian's grandson who had fed Fred while she was away said Fred always had one of her gardening shoes with him on the mat by the front door. With a short bark he seemed to understand as he jumped up onto the porch swing where he could survey all the action on the street.

Gertrude smiled as Harris tucked her into his tiny green Miata, backed out the drive and paused in front of her restored house saying, "Look how the late afternoon sun makes it glow."

"The shadows make it look like an Impressionist painting," Gert added admirably. "And even if I can't see it from this angle, the roof is beautiful too."

"You made a good decision," he said as he drove on, "The ad will be spectacular."

"It has been all summer since I have seen the girls," Gert commented, "And they would be there tonight."

It promised to be an exciting evening.

They had almost reached the Bluff when Maude's van over took them beeping its horn with Lillian waving and pointing to a large white envelope, mouthing, "My book, my book."

By the time they parked, people were being ushered through pine shaded lanes toward the clubhouse. A wide deck surrounded the glass enclosed meeting room cantilevered out over the bluff. Upon entering the room Gert had the feeling of being aboard a ship with an uninterrupted view of the ocean. A microphone was set up in front of a wide fireplace banked in flowers with a bar and a band to one side.

Taking their seats Gert signaled to Maude and Lillian, "Tell me later," and smiled pointing to Howard and Phyllis seated nearby. She hoped that Stella would be here tonight. It had been a tough summer for Stella. Although her news had not been good, the breast cancer was detected early and they hoped surgery followed by radiation had taken care of it. It was here Stella suggested that they meet tonight saying she had a surprise!

Just before the mayor stepped up to the microphone Gert thought she saw Stella and a cute young man slip into seats a couple of rows in front of Lillian.

Opening remarks by the mayor were followed by welcoming speeches by the board of directors before the ceremonies adjourned so guests could mingle and admire the new village.

The late summer sunset was reflected in the wide expanse of glass of the contemporary buildings between the ancient oaks on the bluff. Guests were free to enjoy music and cocktails as they strolled in the park with fountains and walkways leading to the entrances of the new townhouses.

Harris, a proud father, was beaming as he and Trudy made their way outside through the crowd toward Dean to offer their congratulations.

As they approached, they saw Dean pointing excitedly at the prams sailing close to the bluff saying, "Look at them! I'd love to be a part of that again!"

With hugs all around Trudy answered, "You certainly can be."

As more admirers flocked around Dean, Harris and Trudy looked for the girls and were approached by a familiar looking young man with bright red hair. He seemed to be looking for someone too.

"Are you Miss Gillis and Mr. Graham?"

They nodded, "Yes," and he offered his handshake and continued, "I'm Dennis Flagg, Stella's son. My mom has a surprise for you. Follow me."

"Her son? Red hair? It must be!" thought Trudy. Already surprised and speechless, they laughingly followed.

Without another word Dennis led them down a secluded path to the third townhouse where they ascended five steps to a slab cantilevered over the crest of the bluff. He knocked at the bright yellow door. Trudy looked at Harris quizzically but before he could answer the door opened and there stood Stella!

Flamboyant Stella, with abundant red hair, still beautiful but thin, invited them in. It was a stunning room decorated with lots of color, but subdued colors like those seen underwater. Trudy could see the other girls standing out on a balcony facing the sound. She was enchanted.

Harris noted with pleasure the simplicity of design typical of his son's architecture.

Stella asked everyone to come inside for champagne and hors d'oeuvres saying that she was anxious for her friends to meet her son.

As Dennis passed a tray of shrimp kabobs, Penny explained that her daughter had found a way for Stella to contact him.

"He came immediately to be with her this summer." Penny went on.

"He has matured into a quiet shy boy with a sunny disposition," Stella proudly added, saying, "The recent time we've spent together has healed old wounds and we have begun to have an understanding of each other."

Stella explained that Dennis had become a computer expert and with more information from her, he began a new search for his father. Dennis was a baby when Hector disappeared never to be heard from again but she still had some of his World War II papers. With these clues, Dennis was able to trace him through several states, in and out of rehab, and this week they had received final facts. The official news was that after living on the streets for about ten years he had died several years ago in a veteran's hospital. As his widow Stella inherited a modest amount, enough to buy this townhouse.

"Now Mom can paint to her heart's content," Dennis announced.

"And," Stella added excitedly. "Dean and Dennis have met and Dean has offered my son, the computer whiz, a job!"

With tears of happiness everyone embraced Stella and gave Dennis a warm welcome. Stella explained that Dennis would be staying with her for a few weeks.

"So I can still take my turn for bridge next week. We can catch up then on all our news," Stella added "And Dennis has promised to be my chef."

An unusually good natured Howard smiled at his wife and said, "I don't think Penny can wait that long to tell you her news!"

As all eyes turned to Penelope as she exclaimed, "I am going to be - I mean - we are going to be grandparents!" More champagne was poured for many happy toasts to the grandparents to be, the parents and the baby.

Maude raised her glass and said, "I have one more toast. Congratulations to Mom for the publication of her new book!"

"My book, my book," cried Lillian, reaching for the white envelope she had waved in the van.

"I could hardly wait to meet you girls after the ceremony and show you the new book! After a summer of meetings, editing and rewrites, it is finally here. It seemed a long time but actually it is two weeks early." Fumbling with excitement Lillian opened it while her friends gathered around.

"Here it is - the final proof. I should have the first hard copies for you in a few weeks. Wait until you see Stella's illustrations - they are fabulous. Thanks to your encouragement, it is finally a reality."

"This has been such an exciting evening," Penny remarked, as everyone prepared to leave, "The end to a perfect summer."

"We couldn't possibly have any more news to talk about next week. We'll probably just have to play cards." Trudy smiled.

"Don't count on it," whispered Harris, "Because again tonight I'm going to ask you to marry me."

The End (for now)

www.ingramcontent.com/pod-product-compliance
Lightning Source LLC
Chambersburg PA
CBHW071338130626
46556CB00004B/1933